قبضَ الأسدُ على الفأرِ وحَمَلَهُ بمخالِبِهِ الكبيرةِ وزَأَرَ غاضباً:" كيفَ تجرُؤُ أنْ توقظَني! ألا تعلمُ أنني ملكُ السِّباعِ؟ سوفَ آكُلُكَ!"

The lion grabbed the mouse and, holding him in his large claws, roared in anger: "How dare you wake me up! Don't you know that I am the King of the Beasts? And I shall eat you!"

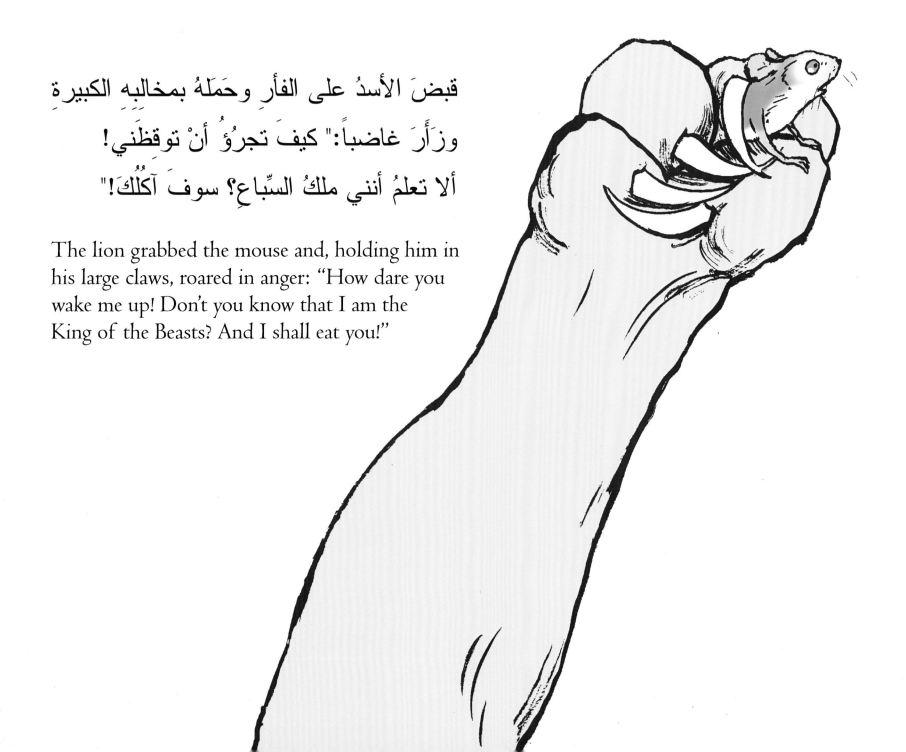

الأسدُ والفارُ

خرافةٌ يونانيةٌ لإيسوب

The Lion and the Mouse
an Aesop's Fable

Jan Ormerod

Arabic translation by Wafa' Tarnowska

منذُ زمنٍ طويلٍ وفي بلادٍ بعيدةٍ، بينما كانَ أسدٌ نائماً، ركَضَ فأرٌ على ذَنَبِ الأسَدِ وطَلَعَ ظهرَهِ حتى وصلَ عُرْفَهُ ثم إلى رأسهِ وهكذا...

استيقظَ الأسدُ.

Far away and long ago, as a lion lay asleep, a little mouse ran up his tail.
He ran onto his back and up his mane and onto his head ...

... so that the lion woke up.

توسَّلَ الفأْرُ إلى الأسدِ كي يُطلِقَ سَراحَهُ.

" أرجوكَ، لا تأْكُلْني يا صاحِبَ الجلالَةِ! مِن فضلِكَ أَطْلِقْ سراحي،
وأعدُكَ أَن أكونَ صديقَكَ إلى الأبدِ. مَنْ يعلمْ قد أُنْقِذُ حياتَكَ يوماً ما."

The mouse begged the lion to let him go. "Please don't eat me Your Majesty!
Please let me go - and I promise I will be your friend forever. Who knows,
one day I might even save your life."

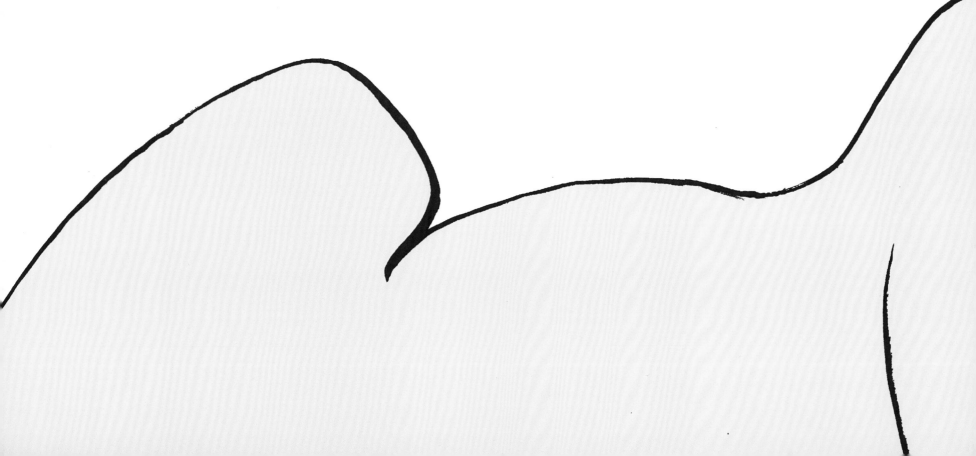

نظرَ الأسدُ إلى الفأرِ الصغيرِ وانفجرَ ضاحكاً.

"أنتَ تُنقِذُ حياتي؟ إنّها لَفكرَةٌ سخيفةٌ! لكنَّكَ أضحكْتَني وصرفْتَني إلى مِزاجٍ طيّبٍ لذلكَ سأُطلِقُ سراحَكَ."

فتحَ الأسدُ مخالبَهُ وأطلقَ سراحَ الفأرِ.

The lion looked at the tiny mouse and burst out laughing. "*You* save *my* life?
What a silly idea! But you have made me laugh and put me into a good mood.
So I shall let you go."
And the lion opened his claws and set the mouse free.

ما كادت تَنْقَضي بضعةُ أيامٍ حتى وقَعَ الأسدُ في شبكةِ صيّادٍ.
ورَغْمَ قوّتِه وحجمِهِ الكبيرِ لَمْ يتمكّنْ أن يُمَزّقَها لِيتحرّرَ.
فأطلقَ زئيرَ غضبٍ مدوّياً اهتزّتْ لهُ الأرضُ.

It was only a few days later that the lion was trapped by a hunter's net.
Even with all his size and strength he could not break free.
He let out a roar of rage that shook the earth.

سَمِعَتْ جميعُ الحيواناتِ زئيرَهُ.

All the animals heard his cry ...

فقَطِ الفأرُ الصّغيرُ ركضَ باتجاهِ زئيرِ الأسدِ وقالَ لهُ:" سأساعدُكَ يا صاحِبَ الجلالَةِ فقدْ أطلقْتَ سَراحي ولمْ تأكُلْني. إنّني صديقُكَ إلى الأبد وسوفَ أُساعِدُكَ مدى الحياةِ."

but only the tiny mouse ran in the direction of the lion's roar. "I will help you, Your Majesty," said the mouse. "You let me go and did not eat me. So now I am your friend and helper for life."

وفي الحالِ بدأ الفأرُ يقرُضُ بأسنانِهِ الحادَةِ الحبالَ التي كانتْ تُقَيِّدُ الأسدَ.

He immediately began gnawing at the ropes that bound the lion.

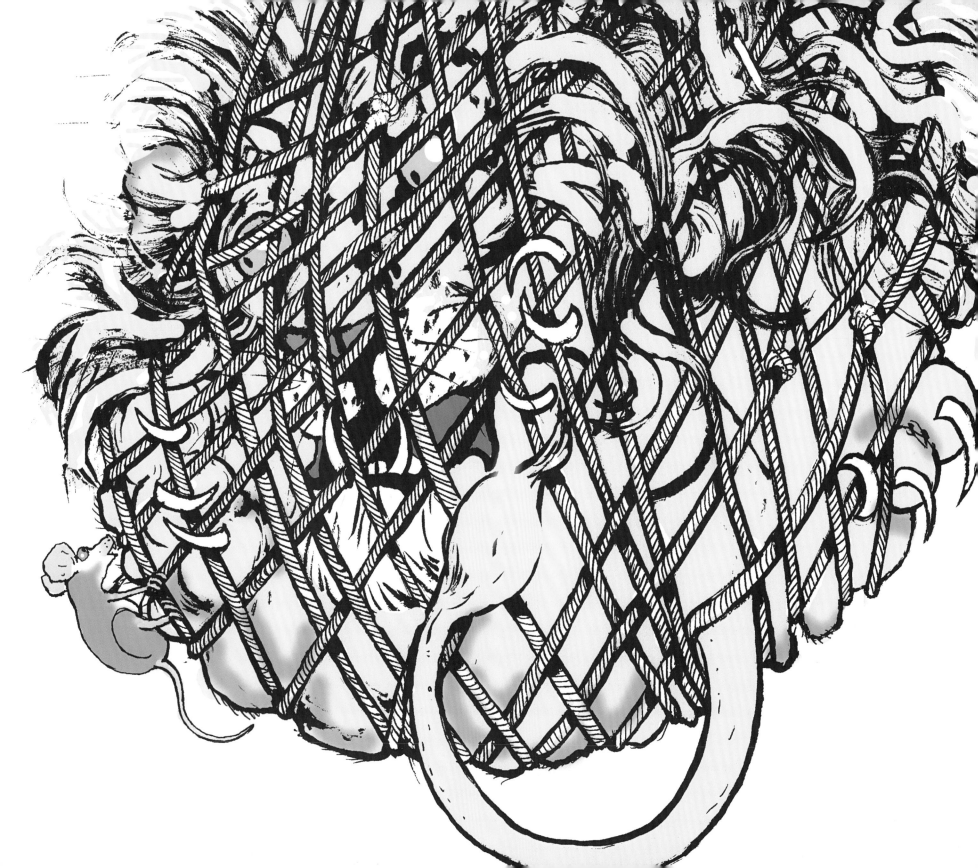

بقِيَ الفأرُ الصّغيرُ يَقضُمُ حتى غابتِ الشمسُ، واستمَرَّ يقرُضُ حينَ ظهرَ القَمَرُ والنجومُ في السماءِ.
أخيراً، وقبلَ أنْ تَطلُعَ الشمسُ مرةً أُخرى، أصبحَ ملِكُ السّباعِ حراً.

The tiny mouse nibbled until the sun went down.
He gnawed as the moon and stars appeared in the sky.
Finally, just before the sun rose again,
the King of the Beasts was free at last.

" أَلَمْ أَكُنْ على حقٍ، يا صاحِبَ الجلالةِ؟" قالَ الفأرُ الصغيرُ. " لقدْ كانَ دوري أنَ أُساعدَكَ."

لم يسخَرِ الأسدُ الآنَ منَ الفأرِ، لَكنَّهُ قالَ، " لمْ أُصَدّقْ أنكَ قد تكونُ ذا فائدةٍ لي أيها الفأرُ الصغيرُ، أمّا اليومَ فقدْ أنقذْتَ حياتي."

"Was I not right, Your Majesty?" said the little mouse.
"It was my turn to help you."
The lion did not laugh at the little mouse now,
but said, "I did not believe that you could be
of use to me, little mouse, but today
you saved my life."

Teacher's Notes

The Lion and the Mouse

Read the story. Explain that we can write our own fable by changing the characters.

Discuss the different animals you could use, for instance would a dog rescue a cat? What kind of situation could they be in that a dog might rescue a cat?

Write an example together as a class, then, give the children the opportunity to write their own fable. Children who need support could be provided with a writing frame.

As a whole class play a clapping, rhythm game on various words in the text working out how many syllables they have.

Get the children to imagine that they are the lion. They are so happy that the mouse rescued them that they want to have a party to say thank you. Who would they invite? What kind of food might they serve? Get the children to draw the different foods or if they are older to plan their own menu.

The Hare's Revenge

Many countries have versions of this story including India, Tibet and Sri Lanka. Look at a map and show the children the countries.

Look at the pictures with the children and compare the countries that the lions live in – one is an arid desert area and the other is the lush green countryside of Malaysia.

Children can write their own fables by changing the setting of this story. Think about what kinds of animals you would find in a different setting. For example, how about 'The Hedgehog's Revenge', starring a hedgehog and a fox, living near a farm.

The hare thinks the lion is a bully and that he always gets others to do things for him. Discuss with the children different ways that the lion could be stopped from bullying. The children could role play different ways of dealing with the bullying lion.

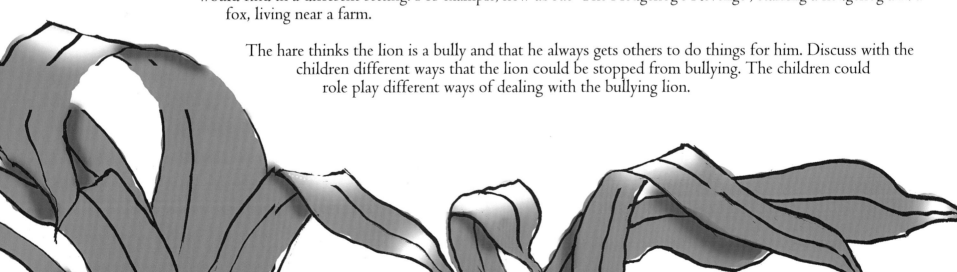

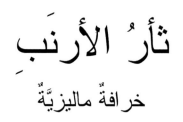

ثأرُ الأرنَبِ

خرافةٌ ماليزيَّةٌ

The Hare's Revenge

A Malaysian Fable

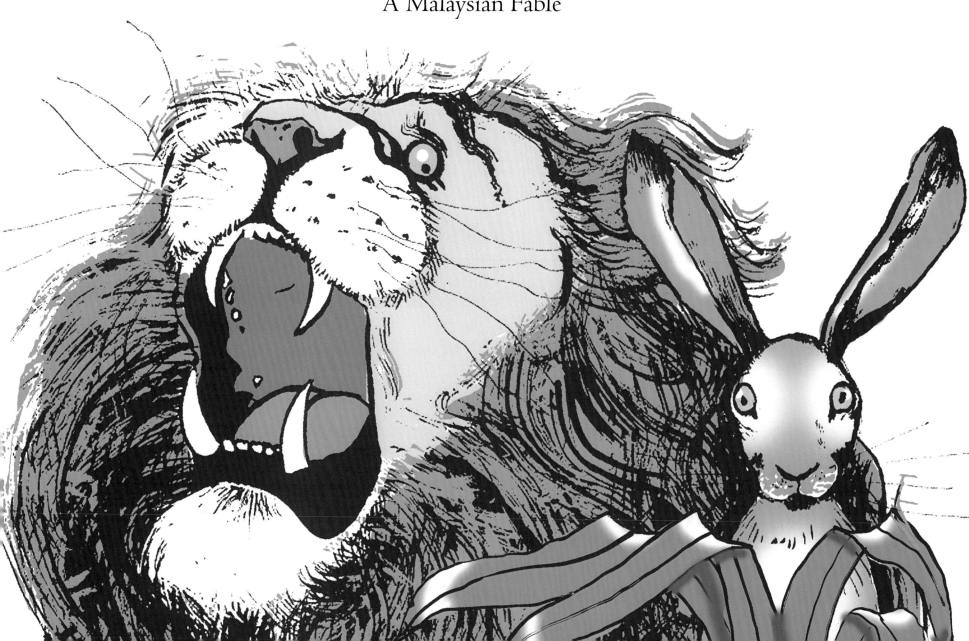

كانَ أرنبٌ وأسدٌ جارَيْنِ.

" أنا مِلكُ الغابِ" كانَ يتباهَى الأسدُ بفخرٍ. " أنا قويٌّ وشُجاعٌ ولا يستطيعُ أَحدٌ أنْ يتحدَّاني."

" نعمْ يا صاحبَ الجلالَة،" كانَ الأرنبُ يُجيبُ بصوتٍ خافتٍ مذعورٍ. وكانَ الأسدُ يزأرُ إلى أَنْ تتأذَّى أُذُنا الأرنبِ، ويهدُرُ هائجاً فيشْعُرُ الأرنبُ بالغَمِّ الشديدِ.

A hare and a lion were neighbours.
"I am the King of the Woods," the lion would boast. "I am strong and brave and no one can challenge me."
"Yes Your Majesty," the hare would reply in a small, frightened voice. Then the lion would roar until the hare's ears hurt, and he would rage until the hare felt very unhappy.

أخيراً فكَّرَ الأرنبُ: "لقدْ سئِمْتُ مِن هذا الوَضْعِ! فهذا الأسدُ طاغٍ وغبِيٌّ وعلَيَّ أن آخُذَ بِثأُري." فذَهَبَ الأرنَبُ إلى الأَسَدِ وقالَ لَهُ: " صباحُ الخيرِ يا صاحبَ الجلالَة. لقدْ التَقَيتُ بأسدٍ يُشبهُكَ تماماً. قالَ لي هذا الأسدُ إنهُ هو مَلكُ الغابِ وإنهُ سيتخلَّصُ مِن كُلِّ مَنْ يتحدَّاهُ."

Finally, the hare thought, "I can stand it no longer.
That lion is a bully and a fool and I must get my revenge."
So, she went to the lion and said, "Good day,
Your Majesty. I've met a lion who looks
exactly like you. This lion said HE
was the king of these woods and
that he would see off anyone
who challenged him."

" آه،" قالَ الأسدُ. " أَلَمْ تذكُرْني أنا لَهُ؟"

"نعَمْ، لقدْ ذكرتُكَ،" أجابَ الأرنبُ. " لكنَّهُ كانَ مِنَ الأفضَلِ لوْ لَمْ أَذْكُرْكَ. إِذْ عندَمَا وصفْتُ لهُ كَم أنتَ قويٌّ، سَخِرَ وتفَوَّهَ بكلماتٍ نابيَةٍ، لا بَلْ قال أيضاً إنه لا يوَظِّفُكَ خادِماً عندَهُ!"

"Oho," the lion said. "Didn't you mention *me* to him?"
"Yes, I did," the hare replied. "But it would have been better if I
hadn't. When I described how strong you were, he just sneered.
And he said some very rude things. He even said
that he wouldn't take *you* for his servant!"

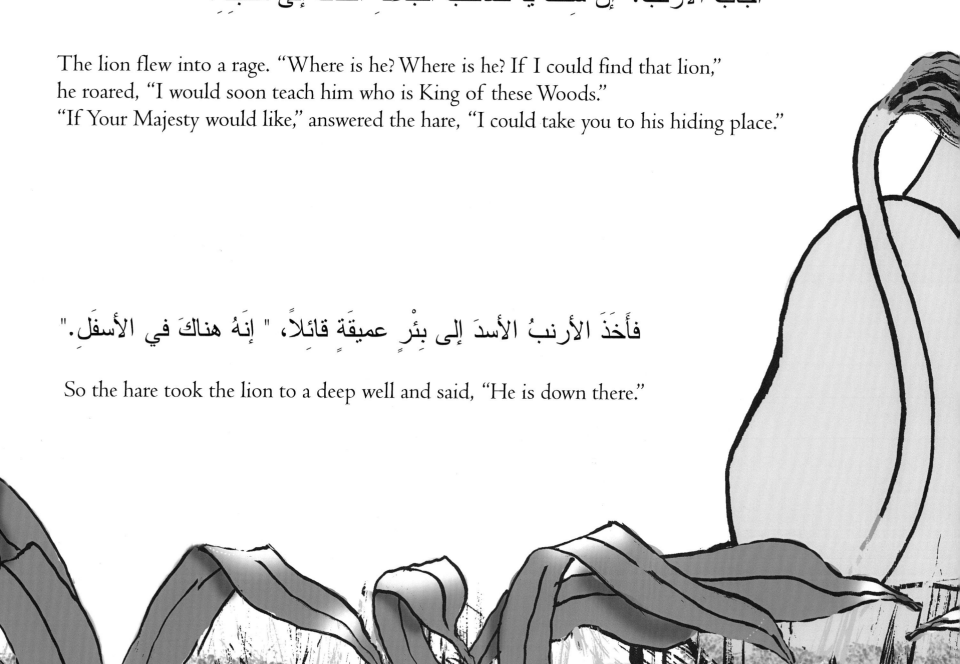

اِسْتَشَاطَ الأسدُ غضباً. زَأَرَ وقالَ " أَيْنَ هُوَ؟ أَيْنَ هُوَ؟ لو عثرتُ على هذا الأسدِ لعَلَّمتُهُ مَنْ هو ملكُ هذه الغاباتِ."

أَجَابَ الأرنبُ:" إنْ شئْتَ يا صاحبَ الجلالةِ آخذُكَ إلى مَخْبئهِ."

The lion flew into a rage. "Where is he? Where is he? If I could find that lion," he roared, "I would soon teach him who is King of these Woods." "If Your Majesty would like," answered the hare, "I could take you to his hiding place."

فأَخَذَ الأرنبُ الأسدَ إلى بِئْرٍ عميقَةٍ قائلاً، " إنَهُ هناكَ في الأسفَلِ."

So the hare took the lion to a deep well and said, "He is down there."

نظرَ الأسدُ بسُخطٍ وغضبٍ إلى جوفِ البئْرِ.

رأى هناكَ أسداً شرِساً يَرُدُّ النَظَرَ إليْهِ بسُخْطٍ أيضاً.

زأرَ الأسدُ فرَجَعَ إليْهِ مِن جَوْفِ البِئْرِ صدَى زئيرٍ أشدُّ قوةً.

The lion glared angrily into the well.
There, was a huge ferocious lion, glaring back at him.
The lion roared, and an even louder roar echoed up
from within the well.

احْتَدَمَ الأسدُ غَيْظاً فَقَفَزَ في الهواءِ وانْدَفَعَ نحوَى الأَسَدِ الشَّرِسِ في أسْفَلِ البِئرِ.

Filled with rage the lion sprang into the air and
flung himself at the ferocious lion in the well.

سَقَطَ الأسدُ نُزولاً إلى الأسفَلِ ولَمْ يَعُدْ يراهُ أَحَدُ منْ بَعدُ.

Down and
        down and
                down he fell
                      never to be seen again.

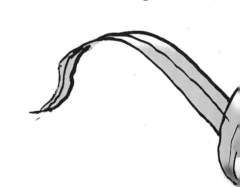

بِهٰذِهِ الطريقةِ أَخَذَ الأرنبُ بِثَأْرِهِ.

And that was how the hare had her revenge.